GEOFFREY CHAUCER

THE Canterbury TALES

坎特伯雷故事集

Illustrated by Simone Massoni

The Commercial Press

Contents 目錄

故事錄音開始和結束的標記
start ▶ stop ■

THE Canterbury TALES
CHARACTERS

The Knight

The Clerk

The Merchant

The Franklin

The Pardoner

Grammar

1 **Read a part of a letter. Complete the letter with the verbs below.**

> ~~am~~ • are • is • know • tells • travel • want

.*I'm*.... reading *The Canterbury Tales*, by Geoffrey Chaucer. Do you (1) .... anything about this book? Chaucer wrote this book in 1387. At this time, God was very important for many people. And people often went on pilgrimages. You go on a pilgrimage when you (2) .... to an important town or city. People go on a pilgrimage because they (3) .... to be near to God. In Chaucer's book, a group of people go on a pilgrimage to Canterbury. Canterbury (4) .... a town in England. Everybody in this group (5) .... a story. And these stories (6) .... the Canterbury Tales.

2 **Put in the right verb.**

> buy • ~~look~~ • study • talk • work • pay

The Knight: ...*Look*..... at the men in the picture on page 25. That's my job. Don't worry! The group will be safe with me.

1 **The Clerk:** I'm a student and I .... all the time.

2 **The Merchant:** I have a business. I .... things, and then the people .... for the things I buy.

3 **The Franklin:** I have a big farm. A lot of people .... on my farm.

4 **The Pardoner:** I .... to people about God. I help them to be near to God.

3 Read about some people from the stories. Complete the sentences with is, do, does or doesn't.

Emily ..*is*.. in the Knight's Tale. She (1) .... young and very beautiful. Who will be her husband?

1 Walter is in the Clerk's Tale. Everybody (2) .... what he says. But will his wife (3) .... what he says?

2 Damien is in the Merchant's Tale. He works for a man who has a lot of money. But does he (4) .... a good job?

3 Dorigen is in The Franklin's Tale. She lives near the sea. But she (5) .... like something about the sea.

4 Ames is in The Pardoner's Tale. He likes to have fun. But (6) .... he a good person?

4 Read these sentences about Chapter 1. Put in the right preposition.

about • at • in • in • to • ~~to~~

In Chapter 1:
We meet the people who tell the stories before they go .....*to*..... Canterbury.

1 They meet .... London.

2 They have dinner .... the evening.

3 .... dinner they eat together.

4 After dinner, they talk .... what stories they will tell.

5 Then, they go .... bed.

Chapter 1

The Prologue

▶ 2 It's a beautiful day! The weather is good. The birds are singing. The grass is green, and there are flowers everywhere. Now, my story can begin. My name's Geoffrey. And today, I'm going on a pilgrimage[1] to Canterbury. I'm going to Canterbury with a group of people. We're going there together. I met these people yesterday, at an inn[2], in London.

I arrived[3] at the inn in the afternoon. I was very tired, and hungry. 'Good afternoon!' I said to the man who worked at the inn. He was the innkeeper. 'I'd like a room for the night. I'm going to Canterbury tomorrow. The road to Canterbury is long. I need to sleep well before I start.'

'Good afternoon,' said the innkeeper. 'Do you know that some other people are going to Canterbury tomorrow? They're staying here tonight.'

'I'd like to meet them,' I said to the Innkeeper.

1. **pilgrimage:** 朝聖
2. **inn:** 小客店
3. **arrived:** 抵達 ▶KET◀

8

In the evening, I met the other people. The inn was big and there was a lot of good food and drink. Everybody had dinner together. And the innkeeper gave good food to everybody. The innkeeper was a nice person. He was a very big man and he enjoyed speaking to people. He was very good at his job. Everybody enjoyed their dinner.

After dinner, the innkeeper spoke to the group. 'You're a very nice group of people,' he said. 'I know that God will listen to your prayers[1]. You're all going to the same place. So, you must go to Canterbury together. What do you think?'

'Yes, we can go together!' I said.

'And I want to go to Canterbury with you,' said the innkeeper. 'Now, we have to travel for a long time. And I think we can do something interesting[2]. We can play a game. What do you think?'

'Yes!' said everybody in the group. 'Tell us about this game.'

'Now, listen to what I have to say,' said the innkeeper. 'We'll go to Canterbury together. And

---

1. **prayers:** 祈禱　　　　　2. **interesting:** 有趣 ▶KET◀

every person will tell a story[1]. I'll listen to every story. Then I'll tell you which story is the best.' Everybody in the group wanted to play this game. 'Very well,' said the innkeeper. 'And I will give something to the person who tells the best story. That person will have dinner at my inn. And I'll pay for the dinner.'

The people in the group were very happy. And they began to think of what story to tell. In the group there was a Knight. Everybody liked him. And he was always happy to help people. He was an important man, but his clothes were cheap. His horse was fast, but it was small.

'I'm a Knight, and my life is very exciting,' said the Knight. 'And my story is also going to be exciting. It's about two brothers who love the same woman.'

There was also a Clerk in the group. He was a nice man, but he didn't speak very much. He liked reading and studying. That's all he wanted to do. He was very slim and he didn't eat very much. And he liked books more than food.

---

1. story: 故事 ▶KET◀

'I read a lot of books,' said the Clerk. 'I don't want nice clothes or good food. I don't have much money. And I use the money I have to buy books. That's why I read a lot of stories. My story is very easy to understand. But, it's not boring. I think everybody will enjoy it. It's about a king[1] who has many secrets[2].'

Another[3] person in the group was a Merchant. He had a lot of money. But he wasn't a happy man. He always had a sad face. He was different from the Knight. His clothes were very expensive. Everything he had was expensive, his clothes, his hat, and his horse.

'I have an important business,' said the Merchant. 'And I have a lot of things to do. But I'm not very happy with my life. And that's why my story will be sad. It'll be about an old man who can't see.'

I also have to tell you about another man. He was a Franklin. He was different from the Clerk. He was very rich[4] and important, but he didn't have a business. He had a big house in the country.

---

1. **king:** 國王 ▶KET◀
2. **secrets:** 秘密
3. **another:** 另一 ▶KET◀

4. **rich:** 富有 ▶KET◀

And he often invited people there. He liked good food.

'I'm very old. And my house is big. And I like inviting people there,' said the Franklin. 'In my house, I often tell stories. I enjoy it. My story will be very interesting. It's about a woman who doesn't like the sea. Why doesn't she like the sea? Well, you'll have to listen to my story.'

There is another person I want to tell you about. He was a Pardoner. He also liked reading. And he liked to sing songs and say prayers. He had a strange[1] face.

'I travel a lot and I always say prayers for people,' said the Pardoner. 'There are a lot of bad people in the world. I'll say a prayer for them, but they have to give me some money. My story will be about three people who do something very bad.'

Everybody was tired. It was late in the evening, and the Knight said, 'We can go to bed now. Then we can leave early in the morning.' We all went to bed. We were tired, but happy.

Early next morning, we got up. And then we

---

1. strange: 奇怪 ▶KET◀

left for Canterbury on our horses. We were slow. And after many hours we came to a place called Saint Thomas. And we stopped there.

We sat down. And then we had something to eat. After eating, the innkeeper said, 'Listen, do you remember what we said last night?'

'Of course,' said the Knight.

'Well,' said the innkeeper, 'who wants to begin? Who wants to tell the first story?'

'I'm happy to tell you my story,' said the Knight. 'I think you'll enjoy it. It's very exciting.'

And then the Knight began to tell his story.

After-reading Activities

Reading

1 Match the descriptions of each story.

    ☑ The Pardoner's story will be about three men

1 ☐ The Franklin's story will be about a woman

2 ☐ The Knight's story will be about two brothers

3 ☐ The Merchant's story will be about an old man

4 ☐ The Clerk's story will be about a king

a who doesn't like the sea

b who do something very bad

c who love the same woman

d who has many secrets

e who can't see

Writing

2 Complete the sentences, using some of the adjectives from Chapter 1.

bad • big • expensive • fast • hungry • old • slim

    Geoffrey was very tired and ...._hungry_... .

1 The Knight's horse was ....

2 The Clerk didn't eat very much, and he was very

    ....

3 The Merchant's horse was very ....

4 The Franklin was an .... man.

5 The Franklin had a .... house.

6 The Pardoner said that there are a lot of .... people in the world.

Grammar

3 Put the words in brackets ( ) into the contracted form.

'I _'m going_ on a pilgrimage.' (am going)

1 'They .... here tonight.' (are staying)

2 'I................. to meet them.' (would like)

3 'You .... a very nice group of people.' (are)

4 'We................. to Canterbury together.' (will go)

5 He .... very much. (did not speak)

6 'I................. happy to tell you a story.' (am)

Before-reading Activities

The Knight's Tale

'My story is going to be exciting. It's about two brothers who love the same woman.'

4 Look at the picture on page 21. Complete the sentences with the words can, or can't.

The man is in a place where he (1) .... go out.
He (2) .... see the woman, but he (3) .... go into the garden.

Listening

5 Listen to the first part of Chapter 2. Cross out the incorrect options.

The knight / _the merchant_ told the first story.

1 The two brothers were clerks / knights.

2 They were from Thebes / Athens.

3 They were happy / sad.

4 They lived in Thebes / Athens.

Chapter 2

The Knight's Tale

▶ 3 "My story is about two brothers," said the Knight. "Their names were Palamon and Arcite, and they were knights. The brothers were from a city called Thebes. They did everything together. They weren't only brothers; they were also friends. But they were very sad."

"They were sad because they didn't live in Thebes any more. They lived in Athens. And they didn't live in a house; they lived in a prison[1]. They couldn't leave the prison and they couldn't speak to anybody. Every morning, they looked out of the prison window. From their window, they could see a beautiful garden." ■

▶ 4 One morning, Palamon woke up and then he looked out of the window. But something was different. There was a woman in the garden. Her name was Emily. She was the daughter of the King of Athens.

1. prison: 監獄

18

'Look!' said Palamon. 'That woman is beautiful. Oh! I'm in love! Arcite! Come here! Look!'

Arcite went to the window. And he saw the woman. 'Yes, you're right. She is beautiful,' he said. 'One day, I'll marry[1] her.'

'I saw her first!' said Palamon. 'You can't love her. You must help me!'

'No!' said Arcite. 'My love is perfect[2]. You must help me!'

Arcite and Palamon both loved Emily. And they had the same conversation every day. 'I love her!' No! You can't love her!' was all you could hear; from the small room, their prison.

And then, one day, a friend of Arcite's visited the King of Athens. He wanted to speak to the king about Arcite. 'Can he go home?' asked Arcite's friend. 'He's a good man. And I want to see him again.'

'I'll do what you ask,' said the king. 'Arcite can go home. But he must never come to Athens again. And Palamon must stay in prison.'

Arcite went back to Thebes. But he wasn't happy. 'I'm going home,' thought Arcite. 'But, I

1. **marry:** 迎娶   2. **perfect:** 完美 ▶KET◀

19

can't see Emily. Palamon can see her in the garden. It's better in prison.'

But Palamon was sad as well. 'Arcite, you can go back to Athens,' he thought. 'You can fight[1] the King of Athens, and you can marry Emily. I have to stay in this prison.'

In Thebes, Arcite was very sad; he didn't sleep, or eat very much. 'I'll wait for two years,' thought Arcite. 'And then I'll go to Athens again. Nobody will know me. I'll wear different clothes. I'll change my name. And I'll find a job. I'll be a servant[2] in the king's house. And then I'll see Emily.'

And that's why, after two years, Arcite went back to Athens. And soon he was the king's servant. The king liked Arcite because he was good at his job. One day, Arcite went to a forest[3] near Athens. And he sat near a tree. 'What can I do?' said Arcite. 'I'm the king's servant. I'm near Emily. But she doesn't know who I am. I want to die!'

Then a man spoke to Arcite. It was Palamon! 'Hello brother! It's me!' said Palamon. 'Stop thinking about Emily! Only I can love her.'

1. **fight:** 打架
2. **servant:** 僕人

3. **forest:** 森林 ▶KET◀

'Palamon, it's you!' said Arcite. 'Why aren't you in prison?'

'The king sent me home yesterday. But I'm not going home. I want to find Emily.'

'Well, I'll fight you for Emily,' said Arcite. 'But not today. We're knights remember? We must do things in the right way. Tonight, I'll bring[1] some food. And then tomorrow we'll fight.'

'Alright,' said Palamon. And so the brothers said goodbye. On the next day, they met in the forest. And then they started fighting.

On the same day, the king was also in the forest. He was with Emily. And he saw Palamon and Arcite. 'Stop!' said the king. 'What are you doing? Stop now!'

'Kill[2] us!' said Arcite. 'Now, I'm your servant. And before that I was in your prison. My name is Arcite. And this is my brother Palamon. We're fighting because we both love Emily.'

'Then, you must die!' said the king.

But Emily stopped the king. 'Please don't kill them!' she said. 'They're fighting for love.'

---

1. bring: 攜帶 ▶KET◀   **2. kill:** 殺死

'Well,' said the king. 'You're right Emily. But only one of them can marry you. Palamon, Arcite, come back to the forest next summer. Bring a hundred knights. And then you'll fight for Emily. Now, go!'

Soon it was summer. Palamon and Arcite came back to Athens. They both had a hundred knights. And they were ready to fight the next day.

That night, Palamon had a dream[1]. In his dream a woman said, *'I can see you. You are marrying Emily.'*

On the same night, Arcite also had a dream. In his dream a man said, *'I can hear you. You are saying, Hooray! Emily will be my wife.'*

Which dream was right? Well, now I'll tell you.

In the morning, everybody came to the forest. The knights were ready and they began to fight!

After three hours, Emily was worried. 'They're fighting for me! Who's going to be my husband? When will they stop?'

And then, after many hours, they did stop. Palamon was very tired. 'Stop!' he said. 'I can't fight any more!'

---

1. **dream:** 夢 ▶KET◀

'Stop fighting!' said the king. 'Arcite will be Emily's husband.'

'Hooray!' said Arcite. 'I'm very happy. Emily will be my wife. I must go to her and,...but then, Arcite stopped speaking. He didn't feel well.

People came to help Arcite. 'I'm not well,' said Arcite. 'I can't, … I can't feel anything. I'm dying. This is the end. Goodbye Emily, my love. Goodbye Palamon, my brother.'

And then, Arcite died.

❖ ❖ ❖

Soon, it was winter. And the king called for Palamon and Emily.

'As you know, Arcite died last summer, and it was very sad,' said the king. 'Emily, I want you to be happy. Palamon, you must marry Emily. It's the right thing to do.'

'Thank you!' said Palamon. 'Arcite was a good knight. He was my dear brother. But, we had to fight for love. Emily, I know we'll be happy together. But we'll never forget my brother. He died for love.' ◼

Reading

1a **Read again about Arcite and Palamon's dreams. Put Arcite or Palamon's name in the gap.**

1 'I can see you after the fight. You are marrying Emily.'
....

2 'I can hear you after the fight. You are saying, Hooray! Emily will be my wife.' ....

1b **Which dream was right? Tick (✓) the correct statement.**

1 ☐ Palamon's dream was right and Arcite's dream was wrong.

2 ☐ Arcite's dream was right and Palamon's dream was wrong.

3 ☐ Both dreams were right.

2 **Read the sentences and cross out the incorrect words.**

Palamon looked out of the window and / ~~because~~ he saw Emily.

1 Arcite went home because / but Palmon stayed in prison.

2 Palamon couldn't leave the prison because / and he was very sad about this.

3 In Thebes, Arcite was sad because / and he didn't eat, drink or sleep very much.

4 Arcite waited for two years in Thebes. And / Because then he went back to Athens.

5 In Athens, Arcite worked for the king and / but the king liked Arcite very much.

6 Arcite went to the forest but / because he didn't know that Palamon was there.

Writing

3 **Read this conversation between Arcite and Palamon in the forest. Put the verbs in the correct form.**

Arcite: I ..*stayed*.. (stay) in Thebes for two years. And then I came back to Athens. I didn't (1) .... (eat) very much in Thebes. I (2) .... (be) very sad.
Palamon: Did you (3) .... (come) back for Emily?
Arcite: Yes I did. Now I (4) .... (work) for the king. He (5) .... (not know) my real name. I often think of Emily. I love her.
Palamon: That's why I'm in the forest.

Before-reading Activities

The Clerk's Tale

'My story is about a king who has many secrets.'

4 **Look at the picture on page 33. Complete the sentences with the words is, or isn't.**

The woman (1) .... in her room. The man (2) .... taking the children. The woman (3) .... happy about this.

Listening

▶ 5 **5** **Look at these sentences. Listen to the first part of Chapter 3. Tick (✓) the ones that are true.**

☑ This is a story about a king called Walter.
1 ☐ Walter wanted to marry Griselda.
2 ☐ Everybody knew this.
3 ☐ Griselda had a lot of money.
4 ☐ Griselda lived with her father.

Chapter 3

The Clerk's Tale

▶ 5 The Clerk was the next person to tell his story. "I have an interesting story," he said. "It's about a king called Walter. He was the king of Saluce, in Italy. Walter wanted to marry a woman. But only he knew the name of this woman. It was his secret. The woman's name was Griselda. She was young and beautiful and she was very nice. She was very poor and she lived in a small house with her father. She cooked and cleaned for him every day. And now I'll tell you their story," said the Clerk. ■

▶ 6 One day, Griselda was at home with her father. 'Today is the day,' said Griselda. 'Today we'll know the name of the king's wife. Who will it be? It's very exciting.'

'I think his wife will be a rich woman,' said Griselda's father. But Griselda's father was wrong. And soon he heard somebody at the door. Griselda's father opened the door. And he saw Walter, the King of Saluce.

'I want to speak to you. I want to marry Griselda,' said Walter.

'Griselda? M-m-m-my Griselda?' said the father. 'But this is strange. We're poor. And you're the king. Why do you want a poor wife?'

'That's not important,' said Walter. 'She's the woman I love. Can I speak to her?'

'Well, of course,' said the father.

And then Walter went inside the house. And he spoke to Griselda. 'Griselda,' said Walter. 'Will you be my wife? You must do everything I say.'

'I'm too poor for you,' said Griselda. 'I cook and clean. I work hard. I have a different kind of life. But, I want you to be happy. I'll be your wife. And I promise¹ to do everything you say.'

'That's good!' said Walter. And then Griselda went home with Walter. Servants arrived. They gave Griselda a beautiful dress. And on that day, Walter married Griselda.

Walter and Griselda were very happy. The people of the city liked her. Soon, Griselda had a beautiful baby girl. Walter was also happy. But he was worried

---

1. promise: 答應

about something, 'Griselda is very nice,' he thought. 'But, does she love me? Is she only nice because I'm the king? I have to know that she loves me.' Then, Walter did something very bad.

One night, Griselda was in her room. She was with her daughter. Walter's servant came into the room. 'I'm sorry, it's late,' said the servant. 'But I must do what the king says. I must take your daughter.'

The servant took the child from Griselda. Griselda was very worried. 'What's he going to do with my daughter? Is he going to kill her?' thought Griselda. But Griselda said nothing. 'Now go!' said Griselda to the servant. 'And do what the king says.'

Then the servant took the child to Walter. 'Don't tell anybody about this,' said Walter to his servant. 'Go with my daughter to Milan. She'll live with my sister. But remember! It's a secret. Nobody must know that this girl is my daughter.' And then the king's servant took the child to Milan.

What did Griselda do? Did she hate[1] her husband? The answer to this question is no. Griselda didn't change.

1. **hate:** 憎恨 ▶KET◀

'Does Griselda love me or not,' thought the king. 'Oh, I don't know!'

❖❖❖

After five years, Griselda had another baby. It was a boy. Griselda was happy again. But Walter wasn't happy. 'Griselda,' said Walter. 'Do you promise that you'll always love me?'

'Yes I do,' said Griselda. 'I'm your wife. And I left my old life. I left my house, and my father. I'll die for you. Is that what you want?'

But Walter wasn't happy. 'I have to know that she loves me,' he thought.

Soon, Griselda's son was two years old. One night, Griselda was in her room. She was with her son. Then, the servant came into her room again.

'I must take your son,' he said. 'It's what the king wants.'

'First my daughter, and now my son,' thought Griselda. 'Oh, my children! What will Walter do to my son?' Griselda said goodbye to her son. And then the servant took the child to Walter.

'Take my son to Bologna,' said Walter. 'And remember, this must be a secret.' And then the servant left. He took the boy to a family in Bologna. 'Now I'll know,' thought the King. 'Will Griselda love me now?'

But Griselda didn't change. She didn't hate Walter. She was good to him. 'I don't know what Walter is thinking,' thought Griselda. I promised to love him. And I will love him. But why does he do these bad things?'

❖ ❖ ❖

For some years, Walter was happy. His daughter was in Milan. And she was now 18 years old. And Walter began to worry again. 'Does Griselda love me?' he thought again. And then he did another bad thing. The king called for Griselda, and he said to her, 'I don't need you any more. I want a new wife.' Griselda said nothing. And then she left Walter's room.

Walter then spoke to his servant. 'Bring me my son and daughter,' he said. 'But it must be a secret. Don't tell anybody who these children are. I'll say to everybody that I'm going to marry the girl.

Of course, I'm not going to marry her. She's my daughter. But nobody will know this.'

That afternoon, Walter spoke to Griselda again. 'Griselda, a poor woman can't be my wife. I was wrong,' he said. 'My new wife is arriving. You must go back to your father's home. Leave your clothes here! I'll give them to my new wife.'

'Thank you for everything,' said Griselda. 'I'll go home to my father. He's old. I want you to be happy with your new wife.' And then she left the room.

The king was very sad. 'I hate doing this,' he thought. 'I love her so much but I must know that she loves me.'

The next day, Walter went to Griselda's house. He wanted to ask Griselda something. 'Griselda, as you know, my new wife is arriving,' said Walter. 'I need somebody to clean her room. Will you help me?'
'I'll be happy to help,' said Griselda. And then she went to Walter's house. She cleaned the rooms. She made the beds. And she washed the plates.

That morning, Griselda's son and daughter arrived. When Griselda saw the girl she thought,

'She's beautiful,' and she thought of her daughter. 'My daughter is the same age,' she thought. And when Griselda saw the boy, she thought of her son, 'The boy is so clever. My son is the same age.' Of course, she didn't know, that they were her children.'

When Griselda saw the king she said, 'That girl is very nice. She's beautiful. Be nice to her. I hope you'll be happy.'

'Stop this!' said the king. 'I don't want to do this any more! My dear wife Griselda. I love you very much! Griselda. You are my wife. And you're perfect.' And then Walter called for his son and daughter.

'Griselda, this is our daughter, and not my new wife. And this is our son. I'm very sorry. I only wanted you to love me. And now I know that you do. These are our children!'

Griselda was happy to see her children again. 'Thank you, thank you!' said Griselda. 'My children are safe.'

That night they had a big party. Griselda and Walter were both very happy. And Walter never worried about Griselda's love again. ■

Reading

1 **Read the sentences. Cross out the incorrect words.**

Griselda ~~knows~~ /doesn't know that she will be Walter's wife.

1 Walter knows / doesn't know that Griselda loves him.

2 Griselda knows / doesn't know that her daughter is in Milan.

3 Walter's servant knows / doesn't know that Griselda's son is in Bologna.

4 Griselda's daughter knows / doesn't know that Griselda is her mother.

Grammar

2 **Read what Walter says and cross out the incorrect words.**

'Don't tell / ~~say~~ anybody about this!

1 Go / Bring with my daughter to Milan!

2 'Leave / Take my son to Bologna!'

3 'Bring / Take me my son and daughter!'

4 'Leave / Have your clothes here!'

5 'Tell / Stop this!'

3 **Re-write the sentences below.**

The tale of the clerk - *The clerk's tale*

1 The name of the woman.

2 The wife of the king.

3 The house of Griselda.

4 The servant of Walter.

5 The son of Griselda.

4 **Put the words in the correct order to make questions from Chapter 3.**

'Can speak I your daughter to?' – *'Can I speak to your daughter?'*

1 wife be Will my you? – ....

2 she love Does me? – ....

3 he Why does do these things bad? – ....

4 help you Will me? – ....

Before-reading Activities

The Merchant's Tale

'My story will be sad. It's about an old man who can't see.'

5a **Look at the people in the picture on page 41 and read the sentence below. Which one is the servant?**

In this picture there is an old man. He is with a beautiful young woman. There is also another man. He is a servant.

5b **Write a description of the servant.**

Listening

6 **Listen to the first part of Chapter 4. One statement is false. Which one is it? Tick true or false.**

		T	F
The Merchant has a wife.		☑	☐
1 The Merchant's story is about a young man.		☐	☐
2 The man's name is January.		☐	☐
3 January wants to marry a young woman.		☐	☐
4 January's wife is beautiful.		☐	☐

Chapter 4

The Merchant's Tale

▶ 7 The Merchant told the next story. "I travel a lot," he said. "And everywhere I go, I see that people are sad. I have a wife. But do you think I'm happy? Well, I'm not happy. My wife isn't a nice person. And I hate my life. I want to tell you a story about a husband and wife. It's a story about a rich, old man. His name is January. January wanted to find a wife. And he asked his friends to help him."

'Don't find me an old wife,' said January. 'I want a young wife.'

January's friends found a wife for him. Her name was May. She was young, but she didn't have any money.

January was very happy with his wife. 'I'm old,' he thought, but now I've got a young wife. I won't have any more problems. And May is very beautiful.' ■

▶ 8 But there was another person who thought that

May was beautiful. It was January's servant. His name was Damien. Damien thought of May all the time. He didn't sleep very much. He didn't want to eat. He loved May. And now, he had to see her every day, with January! Soon Damien wasn't well. He didn't want to go to work any more. And he stayed in bed. In bed, he wrote a letter to May. Then he put the letter in a small bag.

That evening, January went to dinner. 'Where's my servant Damien?' he said.

'Damien isn't well,' said another servant. 'He's in bed now.'

'I'm sorry about that,' said January. 'He's a good servant. He works hard. I want to speak to him.' After dinner, May and January visited Damien. May went to see Damien first. She sat next to him.

'How are you?' asked May.

Damien didn't say anything. He took the letter out of his bag. And then he gave the letter to May. 'Don't speak to anybody about this letter,' he said.

When May was at home, she read Damien's letter. It was a love letter. May didn't know what to do. 'Damien doesn't know my secret,' she thought. 'I love Damien. But he is poor. And my husband is rich. How can I help Damien? I want him to be well again,' thought May.

May wrote a letter to Damien. And then she visited him again. She gave Damien the letter. 'Get well soon Damien,' she said. And then she left.

Damien read the letter. The letter changed him. Soon he was well again. The next morning, Damien got up. Now he was happy. Now he wanted to go to work.

January had a big house and he had a beautiful garden. He often went there. It was his favourite place. Only January and May could go to the garden. January had a key. And he used the key to go into the garden.

One day, January was in his garden. He looked at the trees and the flowers. It was a beautiful day. The weather was perfect. But January didn't feel very well. 'Help! Help!' said January. 'I can't see. I can't see anything! I'm blind¹!' It was very sad. January couldn't see any more. May went to the

---

1. blind: 失明

garden and she took January back to the house. January stayed in his room for two months. He didn't want to go out and he often thought about May. 'What about May?' he thought. 'Now I can't see my beautiful wife. What is she doing? I can't see what she's doing. Does she love me? I know what I'll do. I'll tell her that she must always stay in my house. We'll stay here together.'

The next day, January said to May, 'You must always sit next to me. Then I'll know what you're doing. Sometimes we can go to the garden but we must go there together.'

Now it was May who was sad. Her house was her prison. And she thought more and more about Damien.

Damien was also sad. 'I can't speak to May,' he thought. 'January is always there. I must do something. I need to speak to May.' May and Damien often wrote letters to each other. They wrote about their love. But Damien wanted more; he wanted to speak to May. He wrote a letter to her. In the letter he wrote:

May, take a key to the garden. And then give the key to me. January has a lot of keys. Then tell January that you want to go the garden. Do it now!

Damien gave the letter to May, and May did what Damien asked. She gave him the key.

Then Damien went to the garden. And he waited there for January and May.

Soon January and May were in the garden. January was happy again. 'I'm old, and I can't see,' he said to May. 'But I have you, my love. I love you so much. And I want to show you how much I love you. Tomorrow, I'm going to give you all my money. And this house. And this garden.'

'January, what are you saying?' said May. 'You're the only man in my life.' But of course, there was another man in May's life. And that man was Damien. And now she saw Damien in the garden.

'I'm hungry!' said May. 'I want to go to the apple tree. Then I can eat an apple. Wait here!' But May didn't want any apples. She didn't go to the tree. She ran to meet Damien.

January waited for May. He didn't know where

she was. Now, she was with Damien. But then everything changed.

'I can see again, I can see!' said January to himself. 'How is this possible?' he thought. January didn't understand. 'I must tell May; she'll be so happy.' And so, January looked at the apple tree, but May wasn't there. 'Where's May?' thought January. And then he saw her, but he didn't only see May. He also saw a man. 'Who are you? What are you doing? Leave this garden now!' said January. Damien and May looked at January.

'I think he can see us,' said Damien. And then Damien ran. He was very fast and soon he was outside the garden. Then May ran to speak to January.

'What is it my love?' she asked.

'I can see now. I was so happy. I wanted to tell you. And then I saw you with a man. I think I saw you with somebody.'

'You can see again!' said May. 'I'm so happy. But, what are you talking about? A man! You can look everywhere in this garden. But you won't see a man, because there is no man.'

'I was so excited, that I could see again,' said January. 'I think I saw something that wasn't there. But I thought there was somebody with you.'

'There was no man,' said May. 'Nobody can come into the garden. I want to go back home, my love. Then you can sleep. You're tired.'

'Yes, you're right,' said January. 'Of course, there wasn't a man. Nobody can come into the garden. I want to go home now. We have to tell everybody. We'll have a party. Isn't it great? I'm not blind. I can see again!'

"And here my story ends," said the Merchant. "January was happy. He could see again. But there was something that January couldn't see: he couldn't see that May didn't love him. And that May loved Damien. January wasn't blind any more. But love, is always blind."

Reading

1 **Look at the sentences. Decide who is speaking.**

Damien • ~~January~~ • May • Servant

'Now I've got a young wife. I won't have any more problems.' ....*January*...

1 'Damien isn't well. He's in bed now.' ....

2 'I can't see anything. I'm blind!' ....

3 'I can't speak to May. January is always there.' ....

4 January! You're the only man in my life.' ....

5 'I'm hungry. I want to go to the apple tree.' ....

6 'Isn't it great? I can see again!' ....

2 **Number these sentences from Chapter 4 in the right order.**

a ☐ Damien writes May a letter.

b ☐ January is blind.

c ☒7 January finds a wife.

d ☐ May and January go to the garden.

e ☐ Damien runs out of the garden.

f ☐ January can see again.

g ☐ May writes Damien a letter.

h ☐ Damien goes to the garden.

Writing

3 **Write the sentences in exercise 2, using the past form of the verbs.**

January found a wife

....

....

....

....

4 Complete May's letter to Damien using the verbs in the box.

~~be~~ • go • love • see • stop

Dear Damien,

...*I'm*... very worried about you. You know I (1) .... you. But, we're both poor. That's why January is my husband and not you. You must (2) .... being so sad. I need to (3) .... you again. You're very important to me. (4) .... back to work for January.

May

Before-reading Activities

The Merchant's Tale

'*My story will be very interesting. It's about a woman who doesn't like the sea.*'

5 Look at the picture on page 51. The woman doesn't like something about the sea. What do you think it is?

Listening

▶ 9 **6 Listen to the first part of Chapter 5, and complete the sentences.**

"My story is also about a husband and wife. But, this story is different from the Merchant's story. In my story, love is not ...*blind*.... The husband and wife in my story are in (1) .... The wife's name was Dorigen. She loved her (2) .... very much. The husband's name was Arviragus . He was a knight. They lived in France. But, when I start my story, Arviragus was in England. Dorigen was very (3) .... She thought about her husband every day. And she (4) .... at home."

Chapter 5

The Franklin's Tale

▶ 9   Everybody in the group was tired. It was the end of a long day. They were ready to listen to the Franklin's story.

"My story is also about a husband and wife. But, this story is different from the Merchant's story. In my story, love is not blind. The husband and wife in my story are in love. The wife's name was Dorigen. She loved her husband very much. The husband's name was Arviragus. He was a knight. They lived in France. But, when I start my story, Arviragus was in England. Dorigen was very sad. She thought about her husband every day. And she stayed at home."

▶ 10   Arviragus wrote a letter to Dorigen,

'Don't worry! I'll come home soon,' he wrote.

Dorigen read the letter. 'I don't want him to come back soon. I want him to come back now,' she thought. 'But I must go out. I must try to be happy.'

And so, Dorigen started going out. Her house was near the sea. She often went for a walk there with her friends. And she always wanted to look at the sea. 'Where is the boat,' thought Dorigen, 'that will bring me my husband.' And she sometimes looked at the big black rocks[1] in the sea. 'I don't like the sea,' said Dorigen to her friends. 'Look at those black rocks. They're dangerous[2].'

Dorigen's friends were very worried. 'You must stop thinking about those dangerous black rocks,' they said. And so Dorigen's friends took her to a dance. But, she didn't want to dance. At the dance, there was a man called Aurelius. He loved Dorigen. And he wanted to speak to her. 'Dorigen, you don't know me very well. My name is Aurelius. You're so beautiful. Is there a place in your heart[3] for me?'

Dorigen looked at Aurelius and said, 'No there isn't. I'll always love my husband.'

'But what will I do? I need you!' said Aurelius.

'I'm sorry!' said Dorigen.

'But,' said Aurelius, 'is there anything I can do?'

---

1. **black rocks:** 黑色的岩石
2. **dangerous:** 危險 ▶KET◀

3. **heart:** 心 ▶KET◀

49

'Hmm, well, I want the black rocks in the sea to disappear[1]. Do this, and then there will be a place in my heart for you.'

'But that's not possible,' said Aurelius. 'Nobody can do this!'

'I know,' said Dorigen.

Aurelius went home. At home he said a prayer. 'Help me!' he said. And then he went to bed. And he stayed at home. He never went out: he didn't want to see anybody.

Soon Dorigen's husband came home. Dorigen and Arviragus were together again. Aurelius was at home; he was always at home.

One day, Aurelius read an interesting book. It was a book about magic[2]. 'I can use magic. With magic, the black rocks will disappear,' thought Aurelius. 'I know a man in Orléans. His name is Simon. He's famous for his magic. I can ask him to help me.' The next day, Aurelius went to Simon's house.

'Hello,' said Simon. 'Have dinner with me, and you can tell me everything.' At dinner there was every kind of food. There was meat, fish, fruit and

1. **disappear:** 消失
2. **magic:** 魔法

50

vegetables. They ate, and Aurelius told Simon his story.

Simon listened to the story. And then he said, 'It's true that I sometimes do magic. And now I'll do some magic for you!' And then, the food on the table disappeared.

Aurelius was very happy. 'Can you help me?' asked Aurelius. 'With the black rocks?'

'Yes I can,' said Simon. 'But, it'll be expensive. You have to pay me a thousand pounds[1].'

'That's a lot of money,' said Aurelius. 'But, alright. You must be quick. I want to go home tomorrow.'

In the morning, they went back to Aurelius's house. Simon started work and, after two days, he was ready. 'Aurelius,' he said. 'We can go and see the black rocks.' They went to the sea. But when they arrived the black rocks weren't there any more.

'Oh thank you! Thank you so much!' said Aurelius. 'I must show this to Dorigen.'

The next day, Aurelius met Dorigen. 'Hello

1. **pounds:** 英鎊

Dorigen,' he said. 'Do you remember our conversation about the dangerous black rocks? Do you remember what you promised? Please tell me that you remember.'

'Yes, I remember,' said Dorigen.

'Well,' said Aurelius. 'The black rocks aren't there any more. Come and see!'

When they arrived, Dorigen looked at the sea. And then she said, 'But, how can black rocks disappear? What can I do? I have to speak to my husband.' And then she ran back home.

When Dorigen arrived home, she started to think. 'I made a promise. And promises are important. But I'll never do anything bad to my husband. What can I do?' For two days, Dorigen thought about her problem. 'What can I say to my husband?' she thought. Then Dorigen spoke to her husband. She told him everything.

'Don't worry,' said Arviragus. 'You did nothing wrong. But, you promised this to Aurelius. And that's why you must leave me.'

'But, I love you Arviragus!' said Dorigen. 'Oh,

what can I do?' Dorigen went to a garden. She needed to think. When she was in the garden, a man spoke to her,

'Hello, where are you going?' It was Aurelius.

'I don't know,' said Dorigen. 'My husband says I must leave him. The black rocks aren't there any more. And I promised to be with you.' Dorigen was very sad.

Dorigen stopped speaking. And then something changed inside Aurelius' heart. 'I hate to see you this sad,' he said. 'Your husband is a good man. You and Arviragus have a perfect love. I must stop this. Go home to your husband. We'll forget about your promise.'

'Thank you Aurelius! Thank you! Oh, I'm so happy!' said Dorigen. And then she went home to tell her husband.

Then, Aurelius remembered something. 'I have to pay Simon a thousand pounds. And I only have five hundred pounds. What am I going to do? I'll bring him five hundred pounds. I think he'll understand.'

Aurelius went back to Simon's house. Aurelius

was very worried. 'Simon won't be very happy,' he thought.

'Hello!' said Simon. 'Do you have my money?'

'I can give you five hundred pounds,' said Aurelius.

'Why don't you pay me everything? I did everything you asked of me, didn't I? The black rocks disappeared.'

'Yes, they did,' said Aurelius. 'And I'm very sorry about the money.' And then Aurelius told Simon everything. He told him about Dorigen and Arviragus. He told him about their perfect love.

'You're all very good people,' said the man. 'You did a very good thing. You have a good heart. And I want to be good as well. You forgot about Dorigen's promise. And so I'll forget about the thousand pounds. I won't take any money from you.'

'Thank you Simon,' said Aurelius. And then Aurelius went home. 'I'll never be with Dorigen,' he thought. 'But I'm happy. Because I did a good thing.'

"And that is the end of my story," said the Franklin. "As you can see, it's different from the Merchant's story. Because this story tells us that there are also many good people in the world."

After-reading Activities

Reading

1 **Read the sentences. Who are the people speaking to?**

> Aurelius • Arviragus • ~~Dorigen~~ • Simon

Aurelius: 'Is there a place in your heart for me?' ....*Dorigen*....

1 Dorigen: 'I don't love you. I love my husband.' ....

2 Simon: 'Now I'll show you some of my magic.' ....

3 Arviragus: 'You did nothing wrong. But, you promised this to Aurelius.' ....

4 Aurelius: 'We'll forget about our promise.' ....

5 Aurelius: 'I only have five hundred pounds.' ....

6 Simon: 'You did a very good thing.' ....

2 **Read the sentences and cross out the incorrect words.**

Dorigen always / ~~sometimes~~ thought about her husband.

1 Dorigen often / never went for a walk with her friends.

2 Dorigen always / never wanted to look at the sea.

3 Dorigen sometimes / never looked at the black rocks.

4 Aurelius often / never went out.

5 Simon never / often did magic.

Writing

3 **Complete the questions and then complete the answers.**

> how much • what • where • who • why

......*Where*........ did Dorigen's husband go?
.....*He went*..... to England.

1 .... didn't like the black rocks in the sea?
.... didn't like them.

2 .... did Dorigen and her friends go?
.... to a dance.

3 .... did Dorigen meet at the dance?
.... Aurelius.

4 .... did Aurelius say to Dorigen?
.... that he loved her.

5 .... did Simon want for his magic?
.... a thousand pounds.

6 .... did Aurelius forget Dorigen's promise?
Because Dorigen loved ....

Before-reading Activities

The Pardoner's Tale

'My story will be about three people, who do something very bad.'

4 Look at the men in the picture on page 61. What do the men say next? Put is or are in the gaps.

'Look! Look out of the window! What ....*are*.. those two men doing?'
'Ah, I see!' said Lucien. 'They .... carrying a man.'
'Yes, you .... right,' said Ames. 'Who .... he? I think we know him. Yes it .... Adranus.'
'Innkeeper!' said Jon. '............ that Adranus?'
'Yes, it .... Adranus died last night. Somebody killed him,' said the innkeeper.

Listening

▶ 11 **5** Listen to the first part of Chapter 6. Circle the right answers.

The story is about two /(three) men.
1 Ames / Lucien talked a lot.
2 The men wanted to find a wife / get money.
3 The men were / weren't friends.
4 The men were in an inn / a garden.

Chapter 6

The Pardoner's Tale

▶ 11 "And now I have a story for you," said the Pardoner to the other people in the group. "It's a story about three men. They were called Ames, Lucien and Morise. Ames talked a lot. The other two men didn't talk very much. These men were very bad. They only thought about money. They were always together, but they weren't friends. Friends help you. Friends listen to your problems. They were greedy[1], and they had no love in their hearts. I will begin my story in an inn. The three men were together at a table near the window." ■

▶ 12 'I'm hungry!' said Ames.

'So am I,' said Lucien. 'I want something to eat.' But then Ames saw something strange.

'Look!' he said. 'Look out of the window! What are those two men doing?'

'Oh, yes!' said Lucien. 'They're carrying a man.'

'You're right,' said Ames. 'Who is he? I think

1. greedy: 貪心

we know him. Yes it's Adranus. Innkeeper!' said Ames. 'Is that Adranus?'

'Yes it is. Adranus died last night. Somebody killed him,' said the innkeeper.

'Who did this to Adranus?' asked Ames.

'Death[1] did it!' said the innkeeper.

'Death! That's a strange name,' said Ames. 'Why is he called Death?'

'Because of the things he does,' said the innkeeper. 'Last week he met five people. And he killed them all. Nobody can find him. Everybody is worried about Death.'

'We'll look for him!' said Ames. 'It'll be good fun. We'll find him, and we'll fight this strange man called Death.'

'Don't do it!' said the innkeeper. 'He's very dangerous.'

'Don't worry! We know what to do,' said Ames.

'People say that Death lives near the mountain[2],' said the innkeeper. 'Don't go near the mountain! Or you'll be the next people to die.'

'Well we're going to the mountain. Nothing

---

1. **death:** 死亡   2. **mountain:** 山

will stop us.' And so the three men left the inn. And then they started walking to the mountain.

The three men walked for a long time. They often had to stop. After some hours, the three men met an old man.

'Hey, old man!' said Ames.

'What do you want?' said the old man.

'Do you know a man called Death?'

'Yes, I know about him,' said the old man. 'But why are you asking me this? Don't go near that man! He's dangerous.'

'Tell us where we can find him,' said Ames

'Nobody knows where he is,' said the old man. 'But people say he often goes to a place. They say that he puts his money there.'

'Money!' said Ames. 'Where is this place?'

'Before you walk up the mountain; there's a very old tree. It's near the road that goes to the mountain. Sometimes he goes there. They say he's got a lot of money.'

'I think I know where this tree is,' said Ames. 'We can go there now!'

'No! Stop!' said the old man. But it was too late. The friends wanted to find the tree.

After two hours, they arrived at the place. And they saw the tree. 'I want to look for the money now,' said Ames. 'Do you remember? The old man said that Death put it here.' They looked for the money, and soon they found it. It was under a small rock. There was a lot of money in a big bag. The bag was very difficult to carry.

'Here it is! Look how much there is! We're rich,' said Ames.

'Hooray!' they said. 'We've got a lot of money!' They were very excited.

'I want to get something to eat and drink,' said Ames.

'OK,' said Lucien. 'We can go to the town and buy something.'

'But, wait,' said Ames. 'Two of us must wait here with the money. Morise, you go to the town. We'll wait for you here.'

'OK,' said Morise. And he went to the town. The other two men waited under the tree. After an hour, Ames thought of something. 'Listen!' said Ames. 'There's a lot of money in that bag.'

'Yes, you're right,' said Lucien. 'There's about six hundred pounds. That's two hundred pounds each.'

'Yes, but I think we can have three hundred pounds each.'

'How?' asked Lucien.

'Well, we can kill Morise when he comes back. Then we'll have more money.'

'Yes! I want to do that!' said Lucien. And then the two men waited for Morise.

Morise was near the town. And he started thinking. 'Well, there's about six hundred pounds in that bag. That's about two hundred pounds for me. Two hundred pounds is a lot of money. But six hundred pounds is much more. Six hundred pounds will change my life. I know what I'll do. I'll kill Ames and Lucien. Then I'll have all the money.'

Ten minutes later, Morise arrived at the town. He bought some food and drink. But he also bought some poison[1]. He put the poison in the drink. And then he went back to the tree. It was getting late when Morise arrived. 'Ames, Lucien, I've got the food and ...' And they were the last words that Morise spoke. Because then Ames and Lucien killed him.

'And now we have more money,' said Ames. They didn't worry about Morise.

The two men were happy. They drank together. Soon the poison was in their bodies. And after one minute, the poison killed them.

"That's the end of my story," said the Pardoner. "The three men wanted to fight Death. They were greedy. And that's why they died. I want you to remember this story, when we arrive at Canterbury. And when we say our prayers."

The others thought it was a very good story. And then the people in the group thought about all the stories. There were a lot of things to think about. And, after four days, Canterbury was very, very near.

1. poison: 毒藥

After-reading Activities

Reading

1 Choose the correct options.

At the inn the three men want
a ☑ something to eat   **b** ☐ something to drink

1 The three men want to look for Death because...
a ☐ they have nothing to do **b** ☐ they want to find some money

2 Where does Death live?
a ☐ near a forest   **b** ☐ near a mountain

3 Who do the men meet when they go to the mountain?
a ☐ an old man   **b** ☐ a friend

4 Where do the men find the money?
a ☐ in a bag   **b** ☐ in a box

5 How much money do they find?
a ☐ two hundred pounds   **b** ☐ six hundred pounds

6 Where does Morise put the poison?
a ☐ in the food   **b** ☐ in the drink

Grammar

2 Read these sentences and put in the right prepositions.

> at • for x2 • ~~in~~ • to x2

The three men were ......*in*........ a bar.

1 The men wanted to look .... a man called Death.

2 The men walked .... the mountain.

3 When they arrived .... the mountain, they found the money.

4 Morise went .... the town.

5 Ames and Lucien waited .... Morise to come back.

Vocabulary

3 **Read what the pardoner says about the three men. Put in the right adjectives.**

> dangerous • happy • old • greedy • ~~excited~~ • tired

"Ames, Lucien and Morise were three young men.
But, they were very bad. They were ..*excited*.. about going to
the mountain. They wanted to fight the man called Death.
But the innkeeper said that it was (1) .... On their way
to the mountain, they met an (2) .... man. He told them
about the money. They arrived at the mountain after many
hours. And they were (3) .... But they wanted to look
for the money. When they found the money, they were very
(4) .... But then, they became (5) .... They
wanted more."

4 **Think of all the stories in this book. The innkeeper must choose the best story. Which story do you think is the best?**

	It is interesting	It is easy to understand
The Prologue	☐	☐
The Knight's Tale	☐	☐
The Clerk's Tale	☐	☐
The Merchant's Tale	☐	☐
The Franklin's Tale	☐	☐
The Pardoner's Tale	☐	☐

The best story is ....
I like this story because ....
....

Canterbury in the 1300s

"There were a lot of things to think about. And, after four days, Canterbury was very, very near."

Pilgrims on the road to Canterbury

Now we can think about our group. They're tired. But they're happy. Now they're arriving in Canterbury. While travelling to Canterbury, they saw villages and towns. But these places were small. Canterbury is different. It's very big. The first thing they see is the city wall. Canterbury is an important place. A lot of people come here.

Now they are inside the city. There is a lot of noise. Canterbury is a very good place to buy things. There are a lot of people who want to buy things that they need. They come from villages and towns near Canterbury. You can buy things in the shops, or on the street. People are buying food. They're buying animals. And they're buying clothes. Some people are speaking to our group. They want them to buy something. But the people in our group don't want to buy anything.

They want to go to the Cathedral. The group walks down the street. There are a lot of inns. After visiting the Cathedral, they'll stay in one of these inns. Then they'll go back to London. But first they have to see the Cathedral.

70

Now the group is walking to the cathedral. There are a lot of other people. They're also on a pilgrimage. People are saying their prayers, and they're singing. And, there it is! The shops and the houses are small. But the cathedral is so big! It's the only thing that you can see. But they have to wait before they can go inside. There are too many people.

The cathedral was an important place. Many people came here on a pilgrimage. In the year 1420, for example, 100,000 people visited the cathedral. People went there to do different things. Today, many people go on holiday every year. Then people went on a pilgrimage every year. It was a kind of holiday for a lot of people. They went to say their prayers. People went on a pilgrimage because they needed something. Some people were not very well. Other people were sorry about something. They wanted to ask God for help.

A bishop blessing the annual fair or market

Canterbury Cathedral

> **Read this again. Make a list of the things that you can see and hear in Canterbury.**
>
> ....
>
> ....
>
> ....

Geoffrey Chaucer

Geoffrey Chaucer is very important for the English language. This is because he wrote in English. Before him, people in England wrote books in French or Latin.

We don't know very much about Geoffrey Chaucer's early life. We only know that he lived between about 1340 and 1400. People think that Chaucer died in the year 1400. This is because we don't know anything about him after this year.

We know more about when Chaucer was an adult. In 1357, he started working. Chaucer had many jobs. He worked for the English kings, King Edward III and King Richard II.

He travelled to France and Italy for his work. Italy was very important for Chaucer, because he could read the work of the writers Dante and Boccaccio.

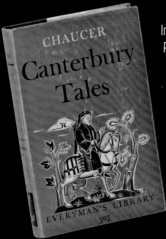

In 1366, Chaucer married a woman called Philippa Roet. They had three or four children. Philippa Roet worked for the king's wife, the Queen. This helped Chaucer to get important jobs.

Chaucer's first book was *The Book of the Duchess*. Then he wrote *Parlement of Fowles*, *The Legend of Good Women* and *Troilus and Criseyde*. In 1387, Chaucer began his famous book, *The Canterbury Tales*.

The Canterbury Tales • Did You Know?

1. Chaucer didn't finish *The Canterbury Tales*. There are also some stories that he didn't finish.

2. Chaucer wanted each person in *The Canterbury Tales* to tell two stories. One story when going to Canterbury. And another story when coming back to London. But they only tell one story each.

3. On page 71 you chose the best story. But we don't know which story the innkeeper chose. Chaucer didn't tell us.

4. There are more than 2,000 new words in *The Canterbury Tales*. For example, the words, 'village' and 'desk', were new to people who read Chaucer's book.

5. When Chaucer wrote *The Canterbury Tales* he lived near Canterbury. But he wanted to go back to live in London.

Read these sentences. Write true (T) or false (F) or don't know (dk)

Every person in the book told two stories. `F`

1. Chaucer worked for the Queen of England. ☐
2. Chaucer was happy when he was a child. ☐
3. Chaucer began writing *The Canterbury Tales* in 1387. ☐
4. Chaucer had three or four children. ☐
5. Chaucer didn't write any other books. ☐
6. Chaucer met the Italian writer, Boccaccio, in Italy. ☐

Food

A medieval baker with his apprentice

The Innkeeper: 'Now, cook, you are famous for your meat pies, with no meat in them. And we know that people buy your pies many days after you made them. Tell us your story.' (From the Cook's Tale)

One of the other people who went to Canterbury was a cook. A cook is somebody who makes food for other people. That was his job. Chaucer didn't finish the cook's story. But the innkeeper didn't think he was a very good cook. Cooks made food for shops or they cooked for rich people. Rich people ate a lot of meat, fish, and white bread. Life was more difficult for people who didn't have much money. They didn't eat a lot of fish or meat. And white bread was too expensive. The cook in The Canterbury Tales had a shop. But most people couldn't buy things from a shop very often. They had to make their food at home. So what did people eat?

74

Breakfast. Most people ate black bread (see picture). White bread was only for the rich. Black bread wasn't very good. It was very hard. And it wasn't very nice to eat. People ate this very early. They ate it at 6 o' clock in the morning. Because then they had to work.

Lunch: More black bread with cheese. Sometimes there was some meat. But meat was very expensive. Most of the time, people ate lunch outside. They worked outside. And they didn't have time to go home to eat. The working day was very long and hard.

Supper. People ate supper before they went to bed. When the sun went down, people often ate soup. The soup had a lot of vegetables. It didn't often have meat in it.

The cook

Read the sentences. Cross out the incorrect words.

Poor people didn't often eat / ~~often ate~~ meat.

1 Poor people always/never ate white bread.

2 Rich people always/never ate dark bread.

3 Poor people often bought/didn't often buy food.

4 Rich people sometimes/never ate meat.

5 Rich people often ate/didn't often eat fish.

Medieval cuisine

Test yourself 自測

1 Choose the correct answer, A, B, or C for each question.

Chapter 1: When does Geoffrey arrive at the inn?
a in the morning   **b** *in the afternoon*   **c** in the evening

1 *Chapter 2:* Where did the king find Arcite and Palamon?
a in the mountains   **b** in the forest   **c** in a garden

2 *Chapter 3:* Where does Griselda's daughter go?
a to Milan   **b** to Rome   **c** to Bologna

3 *Chapter 4:* What doesn't May give to Damien?
a a key   **b** a letter   **c** an apple

4 *Chapter 5:* How much money does Aurelius have?
a a thousand pounds **b** six hundred pounds **c** five hundred pounds

5 *Chapter 6:* Who tells Ames, Lucien and Morise about the money?
a Adranus   **b** the innkeeper   **c** the old man

2 Write the name(s) of the Chapter(s) next to each question. In which chapter(s):

do people go to an inn?   *The Prologue* ....
    The Pardoner's Tale .....

1 do people look out of a window? ....
2 does somebody go blind?   ....
3 does somebody do magic?   ....
4 do people find some money?   ....
5 do people write a letter?   ....
6 do people fight?   ....
7 do people go to a garden?   ....
8 do people go to a forest?   ....
9 do people go to a mountain?   ....
10 do people promise something?   ....
11 does somebody die?   ....
12 is there a servant?   ....
13 is there a king?   ....

Syllabus 語法重點和學習主題

Topics
Love
Feelings
Family
Friendship
Nature
Stories

Grammar and Structures
Simple Present: states and habits
Present Continuous: actions in progress
Past Simple: finished actions
Future forms: Present Continuous, going to, will
Can: ability, permission
Could: ability, permission in the past
Must: obligation
Have to: necessity
Will: offers, spontaneous decisions for future,
predictions

Adjectives
Prepositions (place, movement, time)
Pronouns
Question Words
Relative Clauses
There is/There are
Verbs + infinitive/ing

Answer Key 答案

The Canterbury Tales

Pages 6-7
1 1 know **2** travel **3** want **4** is **5** tells **6** are
2 1 study **2** buy, pay **3** work **4** talk
3 1 is **2** does **3** do **4** do **5** doesn't **6** is
4 1 in **2** in **3** at **4** about **5** to

Pages 16-17
1 1 a **2** c **3** e **4** d
2 1 fast **2** slim **3** expensive **4** old **5** big **6** bad
3 1 They're staying **2** I'd like **3** You're **4** We'll go **5** He didn't speak **6** I'm
4 1 can't **2** can **3** can't
5 1 knights **2** Thebes **3** sad **4** Athens

Pages 26-27
1a 1 Palamon **2** Arcite
1b 3 (Both dreams were right)
2 1 but **2** and **3** and **4** And **5** and **6** but
3 1 eat **2** was **3** come **4** work **5** doesn't know
4 1 is **2** is **3** isn't
5 1 true **2** false **3** false **4** true

Pages 36-37
1 correct words 1 doesn't know **2** doesn't know **3** knows **4** doesn't know
2 correct words 1 Go **2** Take **3** Bring **4** Leave **5** Stop
3 1 The woman's name **2** The king's wife **3** Griselda's house **4** Walter's servant
  5 Griselda's son
4 1 Will you be my wife? **2** Does she love me? **3** Why does he do these bad things? **4** Will you
  help me?
5a The servant is the man in the background.
5b Student's own answer
6 1 false **2** true **3** true **4** true

Pages 46-47
1 1 servant **2** January **3** Damien **4** May **5** May **6** January
2 1 c **2** a **3** g **4** b **5** h **6** d **7** f **8** e
3 Damien wrote May a letter. May wrote Damien a letter. January was blind. Damien went to the
  garden. May and January went to the garden. January could see again. Damien ran out of the
  garden.
4 1 love **2** stop **3** see **4** Go
5 She doesn't like the black rocks in the sea.
6 1 love **2** husband **3** sad **4** stayed

Pages 58-59
1 1 Aurelius **2** Aurelius **3** Dorigen **4** Dorigen **5** Simon **6** Aurelius
2 correct words **1** often **2** always **3** sometimes **4** never **5** often
3 1 Who, Dorigen **2** Where, They went **3** Who, She met **4** What, He said **5** How much, He
  wanted **6** Why, her husband (Arviragus)
4 They're/They are you're/you are Who is it is Is that it is
5 1 Ames **2** get money **3** weren't friends **4** in an inn

78